one HoT summer day

Nina Crews

Greenwillow Books, New York

To my family and friends who have shared my hot summer days

Special thanks to Joy Elaine Henry, who modeled for the book, and her great-grandparents James and Margie Wilson. Also thanks to Donald and Ann Crews for all of their help and advice.

For information address HarperCollins Children's Books, a division of HarperCollins Publishers, 195 Broadway, New York, NY 10007.
www.harperchildrens.com

The art was prepared as collages made from color photographs that were taken and printed by the author. The text type is Franklin Gothic.

First Edition 17 SCP 20 29 28 27 26 25

Library of Congress Cataloging-in-Publication Data
Crews, Nina.
One hot summer day / by Nina Crews.
    p.   cm.
Summary: Relates a child's activities in the heat of a summer day punctuated by a thunderstorm.
ISBN 0-688-13393-2 (trade)
ISBN 0-688-13394-0 (lib. bdg.)
[1. Summer—Fiction.] 1. Title.
PZ7.C86830n 1995   [E]—dc20
94-6268 CIP AC

It's summer, and it's hot.

Dogs pant.
Hydrants are open.
Women carry umbrellas
for the shade.

Hot enough to fry an egg
on the sidewalk.

Well, maybe not.

My mother tells me
to play inside games.
She has the fan on high.

Instead, I stand outside
and tease my shadow.

Then I run into the shade
and draw pictures.

It's too hot to play on the swings or in the sandbox.

I eat two
grape Popsicles
in a row.

Thunder comes,
and then big drops.

I dance in the rain.

I sing in the rain.

I splash in the rain.

The rain stops.

It's nice and cool.
I run to the playground,
and I swing high.